minions

Adapted by Rachel Chlebowski

Based on the film *Minions*

Illustrated by Alan Batson

 A GOLDEN BOOK • NEW YORK

© 2019 Universal Studios. Minions is a trademark and copyright of Universal
Licensed by Universal Studios Licensing LLC. All
United States by Golden Books, an imprint of R
of Penguin Random House LLC, 1745 Broadway,
Penguin Random House Canada Limited, Toro
A Little Golden Book, the G colophon, and
registered trademarks of Penguin R   are
rhcbooks.com   use LLC.
Educators and librarians, for a variety of teaching tools, visit us at RHTeachersLibrarians.com
ISBN 978-1-9848-9733-6 (trade) — ISBN 978- /-593-11908-2 (ebook)
Printed in the United States of America
10 9 8 7 6 5 4 3 2 1

Minions have been on this planet far longer than we have. They're all different, and they've changed over time, but they have always shared the same goal: to serve the most **DESPICABLE** master they can find.

Making their master happy was the Minions' only reason for existence.

Finding a boss was easy. Keeping a boss—

that was a bit harder.

But the Minions never gave up. And then one day, they found humans. This put them front and center for some of civilization's most historic moments.

As the years passed, the Minions bounced from one evil boss to another, never finding a perfect fit.

After so many misfortunes, followed by too much
time on their own, the Minions knew they needed
a purpose—**a villain to serve**.

A Minion named **Kevin**
had an idea: he would set out
to find the biggest, baddest
villain! But he needed help.

Ukulele-playing **Stuart** and little,
lovable **Bob** were the only volunteers.

Kevin, Stuart, and Bob made their way to New York, and saw a TV commercial for Villain-Con, the biggest gathering of criminals **ANYWHERE**. It was their best chance for finding a new boss!

Scarlet Overkill, the world's first female super-villain, addressed the crowd at Villain-Con. She invited everyone to participate in a contest to become her new henchman. All the winner had to do was steal her **ruby**.

"Just take it from my hand
and you've got the job," she said.
Villains immediately flooded
the stage, but they were no match
for Scarlet.

Just when it seemed that nobody would win,
Scarlet found herself holding a **teddy bear**.

Her ruby was gone! The teddy bear was Bob's.
He had the gem!

Kevin, Stuart, and Bob had won Scarlet's contest.

They had a new boss!

Scarlet flew the Minions to her castle and gave them their first assignment: snatch the queen's royal crown. Scarlet wanted to be the new ruler of England!

"Steal me the crown, and all your dreams come true. Respect. Power . . ."

"BANANA!"

Scarlet's inventor husband, **Herb**, gave them some cool gadgets to use for their heist.

The Minions stole the crown! They knew Scarlet would be very pleased. They just had to get it to her without getting caught. . . .

Then Bob pulled King Arthur's ancient sword out of its stone—which made *him* the **new king**, according to one of England's most famous legends.

Bob decided his first act as king would be to make Scarlet the queen. He wanted her to be happy.

But Scarlet locked the three Minions in a dungeon. "I don't want you to take this the wrong way, but I hate you." She couldn't get over their betrayal.

Meanwhile, the rest of the Minions had grown tired of waiting for Kevin, Stuart, and Bob to return. They set out for England to find them.

Because the Minions were so small, they were able
to slip out of their chains. Kevin, Stuart, and Bob escaped
through the sewers and headed to Scarlet's coronation.
Their plan was to apologize and be her Minions again.

SORRY
SCARLET

They found a **wreath** to
give her, and even **adopted a
rat** that Bob named **Poochy**.

But instead of earning Scarlet's forgiveness, the three Minions wrecked her coronation.

This was the day Scarlet had been looking forward to her **entire** life. She sent all her villain guests after them!

Kevin, Stuart, and Bob ran for their lives.

When Kevin finally found a place to hide, he learned that Scarlet had captured Stuart and Bob!

Now it was all up to Kevin. At least he knew where to gear up—he snuck into Herb's laboratory to find something to help him save his friends.

DO NOT PRESS

DO NOT PRESS

After pressing a button on a **strange machine** . . .

. . . Kevin grew and grew until he was **GIGANTIC**!
The other Minions arrived in London as Kevin
rescued Stuart and Bob from Scarlet.

Furious, Scarlett launched a rocket at all the Minions!
Kevin bravely swallowed the rocket, defeating the super-villain
and saving the day.

After Kevin returned to his normal size, England's real queen rewarded him, Stuart, and Bob for returning her crown and defeating Scarlet Overkill.

Kevin had never felt more **PROUD**.

But something was missing.
It was the **crown**. Scarlet had stolen it!
The super-villain was back with a vengeance!

However, Scarlet and Herb were suddenly
frozen by a young scamp with a **freeze ray**.
Kevin and the other Minions were in awe.
They had finally found their new boss!

He was cunning,

he was evil,

he was perfect.

He was . . .
DESPICABLE.